For Brittany and Scott
with love

Copyright © 1993 by Anni Axworthy

All rights reserved.

First U.S. edition 1993
First published in Great Britain in 1993
by Walker Books Ltd., London.

Library of Congress Cataloging-in-Publication Data:
Axworthy, Anni.
Along came Toto / Anni Axworthy.—1st U.S. ed.
Summary: The life of a dog is disrupted when a playful,
tag-along kitten joins the household.
[1. Dogs—Fiction. 2. Cats—Fiction.] I. Title
PZ7.A9616A1   1993   95-52992
[E]—dc20
ISBN 1-56402-172-6

10 9 8 7 6 5 4 3 2 1

Printed in Hong Kong

The pictures for this book were done
in watercolor and pencil.

Candlewick Press
2067 Massachusetts Avenue
Cambridge, Massachusetts 02140

ALONG CAME
TOTO

Written and illustrated by

Anni Axworthy

CANDLEWICK PRESS
CAMBRIDGE, MASSACHUSETTS

This is Percy, who lived very happily

in a house that was all his own.

Then one day a brown box came,

and out of the box came Toto.

Percy went to play with his toys.

Along came Toto.

Percy went to eat his dinner.

Along came Toto.

Percy went out in the garden.

Along came Toto.

Whatever Percy did
and wherever Percy went,

along came Toto.

Percy got grumbly and growly and grouchy. He grumped upstairs to bed.

Along came Toto.

"Go away!" roared Percy.
"You fiddly flea! You measly monkey!
You teeny-tiny, teency-weency,
tiddly-widdly TIGER!
I just want to sleep
on my own!"

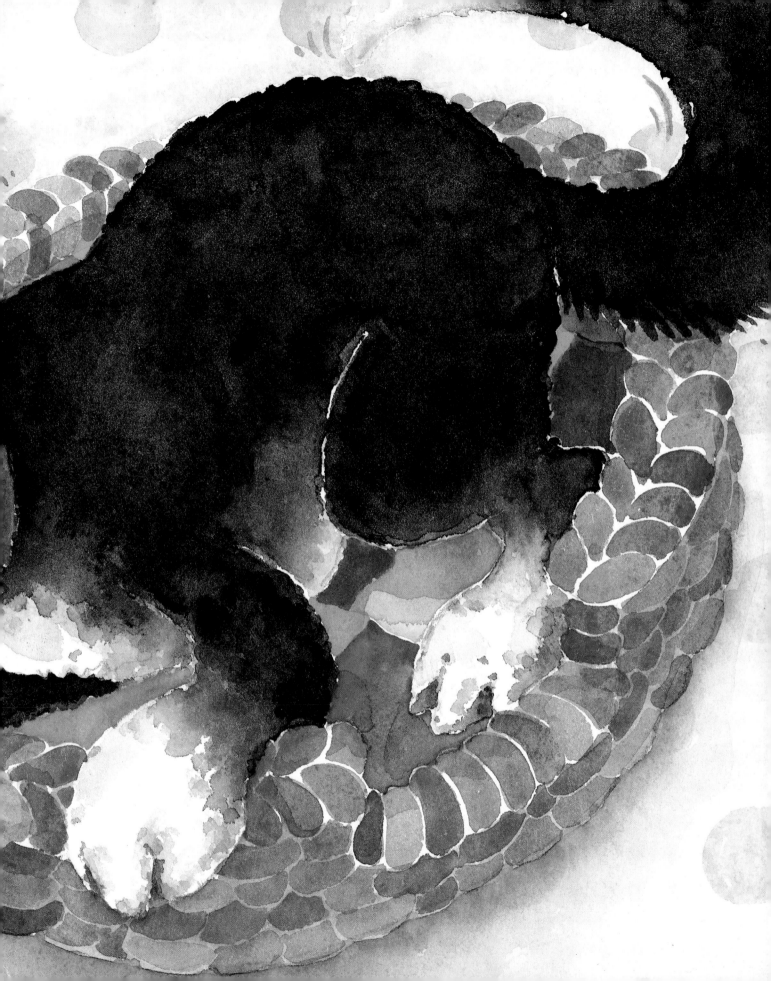

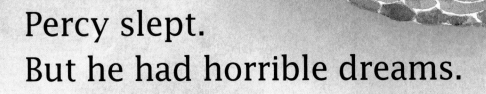

Percy slept.
But he had horrible dreams.

"Grrrrrrrrr!"
roared a terrible, great big tiger.
"I'll eat you up for dinner."

Percy woke up.

"Prrrrrrrrrr!"
Something small
and soft and warm was
purring in Percy's basket.

"Oh, Toto," Percy said,
"I'm glad you came along."